CW00841451

I celebrated World Book Day® 2025 with this gift from my local bookseller and Rebellion Publishing.

World Book Day's mission is to offer every child and young person the opportunity to read and love books by giving you the chance to have a book of your own.

To find out more, and for fun activities including video stories, audiobooks and book recommendations, visit worldbookday.com

World Book Day® is a charity sponsored by National Book Tokens.

First published 2025 by Rebellion Publishing l
Riverside House, Osney Mead, Oxford, OX2 0ES, UK

ISBN: 978-1-83786-414-0

10 9 8 7 6 5 4 3 2 1

A CIP catalogue record for this book is available from the
British Library.

Designed & typeset by Rebellion Publishing
Cover art © V.V. Glass, 2024

Printed in the UK

The SOCCER diaries

ROCKY TAKES THE LEAD
by Tom Palmer

REBELLION

One

Do you have a dream?

We all have dreams, don't we? The dream of a life that would be perfect for us, where we'd be happy and everything would be good.

What's your dream? What are you doing? Who are you with? Where are you? And do you think that your dream will ever come true?

Rocky Race was living her dream. And she knew it. She was sitting on a beach in LA with her three best friends, Kim, Naomi and Mahsa. They'd just finished football training. Or soccer training, as they called it here in LA in California. They each had an ice cream.

The dream. The sun was shining. The palm trees were swaying gently in the warm air. Kim leaned into Rocky, their shoulders touching, feet dangling over the beach café wall.

"When do they get here?" Kim asked.

"Tomorrow," Rocky said.

And now her heart began to beat faster. Because the following day her other friends—her old football team from England, Melchester Rovers—were coming to play a friendly against her school team.

Here in America. Because Rocky lived in California now. She had left behind her childhood home in northern England for American beaches filled with surfers, for a vast ocean, for year-round sunshine. Rocky Race was playing the game she loved in paradise, becoming a better and better footballer, on a pathway to being professional, to becoming, one day, she hoped, a Lioness.

Definitely living the dream. Wasn't she?

Maybe.

Maybe not.

Because the truth was that—even though she had it all in America—she missed home. Missed the UK. Missed the north of England. The Pennines. Skies bruised with clouds. Gusts of wind that poured rain—and sometimes ice—off the hills. So different to California. That life she had lived for the first fourteen years of her life. And the girls she used to play with under those bruised skies. She had missed them. And their arrival was reminding her of that.

"Tomorrow," Rocky said again. "They get here tomorrow."

"Are you excited?" Mahsa and Naomi asked the same question at the same time. On the pitch they were central defenders, the perfect partnership. Always synchronised. They were like that off the pitch, too.

"I can't wait to see them," Rocky nodded, watching a surfer catch a wave for a moment until the board flipped and the surfer disappeared.

"Especially Ffion," Rocky added.

Ffion Guthrie. Rocky's captain back at Melchester Rovers. The girl who—a couple of years older than Rocky—became her mentor and friend before Rocky was offered a scholarship here at Mountain Heights School.

Ffion had given Rocky everything. There had been few opportunities for girls to play football back home. Even five years ago. But Ffion had found Rocky and given her the chance to play in a team. Then she had nurtured Rocky, made her the player she was.

And why?

Because you have as much right to be a footballer as your brother. Because you deserve every opportunity to play football like your brother.

Those were Ffion's words. And they were why Rocky loved her. That and the fact that Ffion was going out with Rocky's brother, Roy. The so-called Roy of the Rovers. A professional footballer for the Melchester Rovers men's team.

"Ffion is the reason I'm here. The reason I'm a footballer," Rocky said to Kim, Naomi and Mahsa, still staring out at the waves, pleased to see the surfer emerge, clambering back onto her board.

Rocky glanced at Kim. "I can't wait for you to meet her," she said. "She's amazing. They all are."

For half a second, after she had said it, Rocky saw something in Kim's eyes. Sometimes you caught the expression on someone's face and noticed something that had not been said.

Now there was a silence. A hesitation in their conversation.

"And she'll love you," Rocky said quickly to Kim.

Rocky saw a smile on her friend's mouth, felt their shoulders touch again.

"If your English teammates are half as awesome as you," Kim said, "then we'll love them!"

Rocky was, in fact, quite nervous about her two worlds coming together, but she hoped Kim was right.

Two

Rocky was talking and laughing so much that she couldn't breathe. Hugging all her old teammates one by one as they stumbled off the coach, looking around themselves like they were stepping onto the moon.

She felt hugely excited. Or emotional. She was not sure which. All the time she kept her eyes locked on Ffion. She had wanted more than the brief tight hug she'd had from her, too. She needed time with her. But that couldn't happen. Not yet.

As soon as the Melchester Rovers team arrived, Mountain Heights School hosted a welcome party for them outside in the eating area, a lovely view of the sun high above the hills as a backdrop. Food, drink, speeches.

That sort of thing.

The Mountain Heights School coach—Abby—clapped her hands once she could see everyone had a plate of food and a drink. She stood there beaming, next to her assistant coach, Jesse, who was also Rocky's mentor at the school.

"Welcome. Welcome. Welcome," Abby called out. "We are so pleased to have Melchester Rovers over here in the States. You are very welcome. And—although you are here to play a game of soccer—you are here as our guests." The former USA international footballer paused. "You need something, just ask."

Rocky watched her old teammates. Some were looking around, glancing at each other. Abby had used the word soccer, not football. How had that made British players feel? Had they even registered it? They clearly had.

It had taken Rocky a long time to get used to that word. Soccer. It still sounded weird. Maybe she hadn't quite got used to it yet.

As Abby's speech went on and she said

soccer a second time, then a third, Rocky caught Ffion's glance and saw a slight roll of the eyes from her old best friend.

After the speech of welcome the Melchester Rovers coach—Serina Heracles—stepped forward and thanked the Americans.

"We look forward both to your hospitality and," Heracles paused for effect, "a great game of… football."

Football. There it was. Coach Serina used the word four times during her speech.

As gifts were exchanged—club scarves, banners—Rocky noticed some of her American teammates snigger. At the word football? Was it going to come to this? A squabble about words?

Rocky knew her American teammates would be thinking that because they were in the USA they would and should be playing soccer, not football.

And on a field, not a pitch.

Also, because they were here, not in the UK, if the score in their game was nil–nil or 2–2 it would be a tie, not a draw.

She would read their minds.

Ffion was standing at the side of Coach Serina as the welcomes and speeches went on. Rocky had not really had the chance to talk to her yet, apart from the quick hug.

But Ffion was staring at her. And not just staring. Ffion was making subtle faces at Rocky now. It was difficult not to laugh. Rocky tried not to look at Ffion. She just stared at a parcel Ffion was holding. To keep a grip on herself.

Then the speeches were over and girls from both teams were chatting to each other. The conversations were about everything. But Rocky couldn't help focusing on the ones that were about words, about difference.

"I can't wait to get out and play a game," Charlotte from England said to Mahsa. "Is that the pitch?"

Rocky had never liked Charlotte that much. She was someone who enjoyed winding people up.

"Pitch?" Mahsa sounded genuinely confused. Then she said, "Oh... you mean *field*. Yeah, that's one of the soccer fields."

Rocky wanted the two groups of girls to

like each other. But there was so much going on, so many conversations she wanted to be part of, she couldn't do it. Not properly.

Overwhelmed, she went to stand with Kim. "This is weird for me," she said. "It's doing my head in." She looked over to see who Ffion was talking to.

Rocky particularly wanted to introduce Kim to Ffion. She knew they'd love each other. Her two best friends in the world.

"Your accent," Kim whispered. "It's different. You sound like that woman on that weird TV show you made me watch, *Doctor Who*."

Rocky laughed now. Kim had no idea what a compliment that was. That she and her dad used to watch *Doctor Who* and that he had loved the fact that someone from the north of England had been the Doctor.

Rocky thought she had the chance to introduce her best English friend to her best American friend when Ffion stood up and came towards her and Kim. But then some of the other British girls began gathering too. Rocky felt overwhelmed again by all the talk and the people. And then Ffion was there and the parcel she had been holding was handed to Rocky.

"We brought you something," Ffion said. "From home."

Kim neatly stepped sidewards, making room for the British girls.

Wanting Kim right next to her, but knowing that couldn't happen just now, Rocky studied the wrapped-up object. She was grinning so much her cheeks hurt. She knew what it was.

Rocky unwrapped it slowly, then held up a red and yellow shirt for all to see. The Melchester Rovers top for the next season. The top she would never wear or play in because she had come to California. She had even missed the last couple of games of the previous season, in which Melchester Rovers were promoted without her.

She regretted that. She had wanted to finish the full season with Mel Rovers. But she had not been able to. She had had to choose. The States or England. The future or the past.

Now Rocky needed to leave the welcome party. To cry. She liked to cry. But not in front of other people.

Three

As THE WELCOME party ended and some of the Mountain Heights girls were messing about with footballs, Rocky and Ffion found themselves alone at last, kicking a ball to each other. Standing fifteen metres apart. Rocky wearing the Melchester Rovers top she'd been given.

"It's so good to see you," Rocky said, clipping the ball to Ffion, then waiting for the return pass.

"You, too," Ffion said, her voice suddenly lower. "I missed you. Lots of us did. But me most of all. It's not the same without you."

Rocky smiled. That was good to hear. Very good. She loved Ffion. Their football friendship. And now she was thinking about home. About what had been going on for Melchester Rovers since she had left. Yes, she felt excited to see her best friend from home, but she still felt like she'd missed out. On the pitch especially.

"What was it like when we… I mean… when you… got promoted?" Rocky asked, controlling the ball, pausing before playing it to Ffion. "Did you have a party?"

"A big one," Ffion said, taking the ball on her thigh and letting it drop to her feet. "But we'd have come top and won the league if you'd been in the team. Not just promoted in second place. Have you played many games here yet?"

"Not since we won that summer tournament," Rocky said, chesting the ball Ffion had played to her and letting it roll down her trunk to her knee, then the pitch. "How's our Roy?"

Rocky fired the ball hard at Ffion.

"He's fine," Ffion said, side-footing it back to Rocky with a deft volley. One touch. "He's hurt his ankle, so he's out for a couple of weeks."

The ball stopped at Rocky's feet. The perfect pass. Ffion still had that touch. That magic touch.

"And Mum?" Rocky heard her voice wobble a bit when she said the word *Mum*. She did a set of six keepy-uppies, left-right, left-right, left-right. Then fired a grass cutter to Ffion.

She missed home. She knew that. But it was made all the more acute now that she was with people who knew her mum well.

"Your mum's good," Ffion said. "She talks about you a lot."

Rocky nodded, keeping her face rigid. It was weird to hear how her mum was from someone else. She felt an ache somewhere inside herself. A longing.

Looking around to distract herself, Rocky saw Kim watching her and Ffion. Rocky jogged to the ball and played an even pass to Kim, who stepped forward and knocked it to Ffion.

This was her chance to introduce Ffion and Kim properly. Her best friend from England and her best friend from the US.

They clipped the ball to each other in silence for a short while. Rocky could not remember feeling so good.

"This school is amazing," Ffion called to Kim. "I wish I was back in California."

"You've been before?" Kim asked.

Controlling the ball, her foot on it for a moment, Ffion nodded. "I did a year at another soccer school. Just a year. Before I went back to Melchester. To be honest, I'm hoping Rocky does the same. A year, then comes back."

"No way," Kim shook her head. "She's staying right here."

The three girls played the ball to each other. Crisp accurate passes.

"I don't blame you for wanting to keep her," Ffion conceded at last. "She's special."

Rocky grinned to herself. Two people who liked her. Two people she liked, too.

Before long their three-way kick about grew. Bored with chatting and legs still stiff from the flight and bus transfer, the Melchester Rovers players joined in.

"Come on, let's have a quick game of soccer," Naomi suggested.

"Football!" Ffion shouted. "A game of football, you mean?"

That again. But it was all okay. It was said light-heartedly.

There was laughter now as at least twenty players were somehow suddenly playing a match. None in football kit or boots. You couldn't tell who was on which side by what the players were wearing, as their clothes were quite similar even though they were from opposite sides of a huge ocean.

But it was clearly Mountain Heights versus Melchester Rovers.

Somehow Rocky found herself playing for Melchester. Since she was still in the new top she'd been given, how could she not? And, as they played, it seemed every conversation hung round the different words each set of players used to describe the game.

The coaches—Abby and Serina—had caused this, Rocky knew, stressing the difference in words.

"What's the score?"

"One—one. A draw."

"A tie, you mean?"

Laughter. Then a foul. Just a nudge.

"The ball's off the field. It's a throw in!"

"The field? What are you talking about? It's a pitch."

More laughter. Sort of laughter. Sort of not laughter.

And now, increasingly, the tackles were flying in. Without a referee, there were sly pushes, challenges that were closer to fouls, a handball, another handball, play carrying on regardless, the intensity increasing.

To the point that there was an edge to it now. A rivalry brewing. Rocky could sense it. And she loved it. Even if she wasn't sure if she should be playing for Melchester Rovers or her school. Which side should she go on? Her old team versus her new team?

At one point, Rocky was free with the ball and running in on goal, Ffion wide of her, and Rocky found she was laughing. Laughing like she was five years old. Laughing so much she could barely breathe in enough air to run with the ball.

And suddenly she was scythed down, a sweeping tackle that took her legs, Naomi underneath, Ffion standing over them both, trying to grab at Naomi. A fight, but not a fight. Then Mahsa and Naomi trying to pull the Melchester Rovers shirt off Rocky.

"Why are you wearing that? You play for us now!"

And then the shout. "STOP IT! STOP IT NOW!"

Coach Abby.

"For goodness' sake. What are you doing? It's all right to mess around, but this is too much."

Silence. Everyone standing still. Like in training, when they stop you exactly where you are and try to explain positions, offside, that sort of thing. The Melchester Rovers players looked really quite shocked.

"Use your common sense," Abby went on, properly angry now, which she never was.

She was so angry, in fact, it was hard not to laugh.

"You are gifted players and to see you risking injuring each other is not a good thing. First and foremost you are young soccer players. Young women who should value yourselves and others. I do not want to see this in the game tomorrow. Am I clear? This is not the way to play soccer."

"Football," Rocky said under her breath, unable to stop herself, still laughing.

But she stopped laughing when she saw the look Abby gave her. A look that felt more like a punch.

Four

THE MELCHESTER ROVERS players had been given a whole corridor in one of the school's newer accommodation blocks. After they'd all eaten an evening meal and had time to settle in, Rocky decided to go and check in on her old teammates, make sure they were okay. And it was an excuse to try to spend a bit of time with Ffion.

She found them all in the common room at the end of their corridor.

"Hey," she said, walking into a sudden hush.

"Heyyyy, dude," Charlotte said back in an American accent. Two or three of the other girls laughed before Ffion stood to hug Rocky.

Charlotte. Again. Always trying to have the last word, be funny, all to get close to Ffion.

Rocky let herself be hugged and closed her eyes, so that any of her old teammates who were watching wouldn't see that Charlotte had upset her. What was that remark about? Were they saying she sounded American now?

Rocky gathered herself. Then wished she was back in her room, door closed. But she was here and she had to be sociable. Welcoming, even.

"Everything okay?" she asked over Ffion's shoulder, careful to use words that wouldn't be seen to be American and set Charlotte off again. "Can I get you... can I do anything for anyone?"

"We're fine," Ffion said, releasing Rocky from the embrace.

"You never used to hug," Charlotte remarked, coming over to put her hand on Ffion's shoulder. "You've changed."

Rocky resisted the urge to push Charlotte's arm away from Ffion. A sudden

26

flash of anger that, on the football pitch, she might have acted on.

"Meaning?" Rocky replied instead, trying not to sound too hostile or defensive.

"Meaning all your American girls," Charlotte said, glancing round the Melchester team. "You and them all hug a lot. They're loud, too. They're American. That's all I mean."

Rocky shrugged. What did she say back to that? She wished she had the strength to say nothing. Reply with a hostile silence. But she wanted to keep things nice, smooth things over.

"They're from other countries, too. Like Ghana, Iran, Canada," Rocky explained, wanting to say that the only thing they had in common was that they were not British, but keeping it in because she had no idea what it would really mean if she said it. Or how Charlotte or the others would react.

"They're great," Ffion said. "I love them. I loved it here when I was over in the States."

Helena—another Melchester player—

nodded. "I like them. They talk like some of the YouTubers I watch."

"And that's good?" Charlotte snapped at Helena.

Helena shook her head. "Charlotte, what's your beef?"

Silence. Rocky was glad Charlotte had drawn criticism from someone else. Someone needed to shut her up.

After a few more minutes talking mostly to Ffion, Rocky came away from the English corridor. She walked slowly across the outside eating area, waving to a couple of boys she knew, then hesitated when she found herself alone. Able to look out across the sports fields to see the range of hills to the north-west darken into silhouette as the sun began to go down.

She felt uneasy.

The idea Charlotte had raised that Rocky had changed. And insinuating that there was something wrong with being a bit American.

She was also worried that when she went

back to her flat, Kim, Naomi and Mahsa might be talking about the English girls.

What would she do? How should she react?

Urgh.

Rocky wondered if she should call her mum. Even Roy? No... no, it was too early in the morning for them still.

Through the door, up the steps, along the corridor. Rocky put her hand on the door to her flat and pushed.

Five

ENTERING THE APARTMENT she shared with Kim, Naomi and Mahsa, Rocky felt tired, but happy. Probably a bit overstimulated, bordering on overwhelmed. But that was okay, wasn't it? Sometimes social situations did that to you. You enjoyed them at the time, then processed them later. That was what she'd learned.

Her three friends smiled and welcomed her back, talking about what a great day it had been, how wonderful it was to meet Rocky's friends from home. Kim led the way, enthusing about Ffion. And the others.

"I love them. They're funny. And they talk like you. I like that a lot. It makes me like them immediately."

Rocky grinned. This was what she wanted to hear.

"Some of them are a bit stuck up, though," Naomi said. "You have to admit that, Rocky."

Not something Rocky wanted to hear. What was it about these two groups of girls that they were always looking for differences?

And should she respond? Should she push back at Naomi? Sometimes you did. Sometimes you didn't. She wondered why she was being so sensitive.

"Do I have to admit that?" Rocky snapped, unable to hold in her irritation after all, anger in her voice. "What's stuck up about them?"

Naomi held her hands up. "I'm sorry. I'm sorry. They're just a bit British." She laughed. Mahsa laughed too. "You know? Like the way they refuse to say soccer and say football like they want you to say it too… and they're so… I dunno… defensive… but not in a soccer way."

Mahsa laughed at Naomi's joke. Then she

joined in. "And soft-spoken. It was like they don't like loud voices. You know? The way they looked at Abby when she told them off. They looked wounded."

Rocky felt her fists clenching and—not liking that feeling at all—started backing away towards her room. Yes. To be alone in her room where she didn't have to react to this, hear this. Where the others wouldn't see her confusion, her anger.

"They're great," Kim intervened, her eyes on Rocky's fists. "All of them. They're just a bunch of girls. And in a place they don't know either. We're all different."

Rocky was still thinking over something Mahsa had said. *Soft-spoken*. And what Naomi had said too. *Stuck up*. What did that mean? She felt extremely and surprisingly defensive of her old teammates. It was impossible not to fight back.

"But *you're* soft-spoken, Mahsa," Rocky said quietly. "You barely said a word the first few weeks we were here."

"I did," Mahsa answered.

"You didn't." The anger and exhaustion

Rocky had been feeling was unleashed now. "And Naomi, you can be so stuck up. Maybe you both see yourselves in them? Maybe that's it."

"I'm nothing like those girls," Naomi muttered.

Rocky spread her arms out. "Meaning?"

A pause. Silence. No one knew what to say.

Except Kim, who took control, standing between the three other girls and—like a referee stopping a fight from brewing—faced each of them down.

"Where has this come from?" Kim asked, not allowing any of the others to speak. "I'll tell you where. We are all tired. And none of the three of us quite like it that Rocky—who we love—has other friends. I don't like it. I am even a bit envious of Ffion. But that's life. These things happen. It's just how we deal with them that makes a difference. It's how we move on, how we accept each other."

Something changed then. The air, the mood, the vibe. Kim had nailed it. The tension drained from the room. Kindness filled the vacuum.

"I am so sorry," Naomi said suddenly. She took Rocky's hands in hers. "Please... I am so sorry. That was so disrespectful of me to your friends. If... I mean, if you had spoken about a group of my friends from Ghana like that... please... please forgive me."

"Me too," Mahsa said, looking shocked. "We got carried away. I don't know how... why."

Rocky smiled, glanced at Kim.

"It's fine," she said. "We all gave as good as we got. I love you girls. I love my life here. This is where I want to be and you are who I want to be with right now. Do you hear me?"

Rocky went to bed feeling a lot better, but still, in the back of her mind, she wondered how tomorrow would go. The game. Was this whole competition between her two worlds going to blow up?

Six

AFTER HER THREE friends headed to bed, Rocky slipped out of their apartment to go outside under darkening skies. A short run to clear her head. This would help stop her thoughts spiralling the wrong way. Then she would sleep better.

Rocky only wanted to do a light jog. Then a few very gentle stretches. Nothing that would deplete her. Loosen up her mind as much as her body.

The sun had set and the sky to the west— over the ocean—was a rich orange, wisps of cloud darkening on the horizon behind the hills to the north. And the air was—at last—cooling. It was lovely. California was always lovely. Whatever time of day.

I'll do one lap of the football field, Rocky said to herself, then stopped.

Field.

Football *field*.

She was thinking in American. After all the banter about words earlier, the realisation made her smile, but also feel uneasy. How weird was this? Especially now.

She was glad to see Coach Jesse on the pitch or field—or whatever it was. In the absence of her mum, he was the one she liked to go to with the knots that formed in her day.

Jesse had a garden fork in his hands and was repairing the grass that had been torn by the girls earlier. It was late to be doing this, but she knew he liked to work the pitch when it was cool and the strong sun was off the grass. He said it helped him sleep.

"Hey," she called out.

"Rocky Race. You're out late! Getting some air?"

"Clearing my mind," Rocky said. She knew Jesse would be pleased, as he was her mentor at the school, as well as one of her soccer coaches. He had helped her a lot, in fact. More with ways of seeing and being than stuff in the classroom. He was there for her to go to, to talk to. Always asking a question to make her think. And this was perfect timing. It was like he'd been sent.

"And?" he asked.

There it was. The question. His invitation for her to talk.

"And... I am finding it pretty weird with both my sets of friends here at once. It's hard to know what to say sometimes, what to feel."

Jesse nodded, but said nothing. He was doing that mentor thing he did when he listened, gave her the space to think and to talk.

Rocky decided to get right to it. She had learned, through Jesse, to be direct, say exactly what was in her mind.

"It's partly how the girls—some of the girls—here have been saying that my friends from home are quiet and, what's the word?" she said. "Stuck up. That's it. And they're not."

"I didn't think so," Jesse agreed.

Rocky put her hands on top of her head, to breathe in deeply. She smiled at her mentor.

"Then the girls from England are glancing at each other thinking the girls here are loud and hug too much. It's like they're looking for reasons to say that they're different, and that that's bad. And I don't like it. Then one lot says I am being like this and the other lot say I've changed. And I don't like being in the middle."

It all came out. All the things she had not thought through yet. Here they were. Laid at the feet of her counsellor.

Jesse nodded. "And you want some advice?" he asked.

"Yes," Rocky said. "Please."

Jesse thrust his fork into the football pitch and leaned on it.

"You're getting older," he said. "You've left your comfort zone. Melchester. Yeah?"

"Yeah."

"And you're on this adventure with new people in a new place. You have two lives now. So, in a way you are two different people. Sort of. Do you think that?"

"I get that," Rocky said. The idea had already half formed in her head even before Jesse said it.

"Take me, for example," Jesse went on. "I'm a soccer coach, a high school mentor, but I am also a father. And I'm a son. And my childhood buddies? They live in a place called Nephi, Utah. Verrrrry different to California. I have to rein in my LA ways when I go home. You have to adapt. I mean... you are quite a different person on the soccer field than you are in the classroom, right?"

Rocky nodded. That made some sense. "But am I being two-faced... or not me... if I change when I'm with different people?" she asked.

Jesse shook his head. "No. And here it's not about you. You behave with one set of people because you are thinking about them and their needs. I talk to my son— who is five—in a very different way to how you and I are talking. I'm thinking about him. Just like I'm thinking about you now. It's to do with listening and kindness. Not just being self-absorbed. Doing what you do is the opposite of selfish, Rocky."

Rocky made to walk away.

"Just be yourself," Jesse said. "You're a good footballer. You can slot into any team and improve it."

"Thank you."

"You're welcome."

BACK IN HER room, Rocky looked at herself in the mirror, still wearing her simple white Mountain Heights training top from the run. She put the Melchester Rovers top she had been given by Ffion over it. Then she took it off again.

Who are you? she asked herself silently.

She thought of the Mountain Heights girls and the Melchester Rovers girls. *Who are they? Which group do I belong to?*

Both. That was what Jesse was getting at.

But Rocky remained confused. Was Jesse right? Could she have two groups of friends? Or was he wrong? He might be wrong. What did he know? Couldn't she just be Rocky Race? Could you do that? Just be you?

She'd find that out. Tomorrow.

Seven

AND SO THE day of the big match arrived. Mountain Heights School versus Melchester Rovers.

Rocky was awake before six, as usual. And, also as usual, she was going to have breakfast early. Alone. So she could wake up on her own terms. No talking. No thinking. Just her and the view of the hills.

She went to shower in the bathroom she shared with Kim, Mahsa and Naomi. Quietly, as always. Sometimes she was up two hours before the others. She did not want to wake them.

But today things were different. Someone had already been in the shower: the mirror was steamed up. The floor was slightly wet.

Evidence from this morning, not last night. And when Rocky came out of her bedroom to head to the canteen Kim was eased back on the sofa, smiling.

"Can I join you?" Kim asked.

Rocky was torn. Did she want this? She hated having breakfast with anyone else. But Kim? Kim wasn't just anyone else. And—to be fair—they'd had breakfast before when Rocky had stayed with Kim and her mum at their beach house. She'd coped with it then, hadn't she?

"Sure."

They walked in silence out of their apartment block, across the school courtyard and into the canteen. Rocky was very nervous that the English girls would be up and at breakfast. Their body clocks would be all over the place. They would still be on UK time.

But they were not there. It was just Kim and Rocky.

The kitchen staff said hello to their first customer of the day as they always did. Rocky waved back at them.

Even though her ritual was to have breakfast alone, Rocky kind of liked it that Kim was there. Kim wasn't talking. She knew Rocky didn't want a conversation. Not in the morning. But, saying that, Rocky did want to know how Kim felt. About last night, about the English footballers. About her.

As it was a match day, Rocky was having pancakes. Five. Piled high with blueberries and a drizzle of syrup. Plus a cup of tea.

This was her pre-match meal.

About to make her tea, Rocky hesitated at the boiling water taps. Should she have tea? She never used to have tea back home in the UK. Why did she even drink tea in the US?

She made two cups of tea, though. One for her. One for Kim.

They sat in silence, eating their breakfast, backs to the rest of the room, staring out at the morning sun, illuminating the hills to the north. It reminded Rocky of Kim's beach house again. The beach house was not far from here, where they'd been a few times. Just empty sandy beaches and waves breaking. Palm trees. Like something out of a music video.

It was peaceful. It was calm. But Rocky knew there was a conversation to be had when Kim started it.

"Can I say something?" Kim asked.

"Sure," Rocky replied.

There was a pause.

Rocky glanced at her friend. Kim looked very uneasy.

"Say it. It's fine." Rocky wanted to encourage Kim to say what she wanted to. "Even if it's a criticism, it's fine coming from you. I can listen to you."

"It's not a criticism. Never."

"Okay."

Another pause.

"I know the different sets of players have been putting pressure on you to be more British or more American," Kim began at last. "I see you being pulled this way and that. Them wanting you to be this. Us wanting you to be that. Play for us. Play for them. But you're you… and that's why I like you."

45

"Thanks," Rocky smiled. "I like you, too."

She actually wanted to say that she loved Kim. But she didn't say it. She smiled at the thought. British people didn't say they loved people, did they? That was the stereotype. Did it mean she was quiet and reserved? Did it mean she was stuck up?

"There's something else," Kim said.

"Okay?"

"I…" Kim laughed. "I'm jealous of Ffion. That she's known you all your life. You know…"

Rocky turned to Kim again. "You don't need to be jealous of Ffion."

"But I am. I can admit it. It's normal. Jealousy is normal, even if it hurts a bit. You have to live with it."

"I've only known Ffion for a few years," Rocky started. "And she's—"

"You don't need to play her down—" Kim tried to interrupt, but Rocky pushed on.

"No, I do," Rocky said. "Ffion is great. She's amazing. I idolise her. She's sort of my hero. But you and me… We're on a level. We're friends. I've never had a friend like you."

Kim grinned. Rocky figured she'd said the right thing. Then—after a pause—she asked, "So, if it comes up and becomes... you know... if someone asks you who are you going to play for?"

Rocky rolled her eyes, then had an idea. It came into her head right then. It was as if the conversation they were having now had formed it.

Rocky looked into her friend's eyes. "I've got a plan."

"A plan?"

"Yes. So we all forget the things that make us different, realise what we have in common."

"Sounds great," Kim smiled. "Whatever it is."

"I'm glad you said that," Rocky declared. "Because I'd like to ask if you would be part of it?"

Eight

THE PRE-MATCH ATMOSPHERE was building. Students from Mountain Heights School gathered on the bleachers to watch. Rocky could hear them. She saw them, too. Saw that some had American flags. So, it was going to be like that, was it?

Okay.

Knowing both teams would be heading for the changing rooms soon, Rocky went to find Abby. She had something she wanted to run by her coach. An idea. Her plan.

After her chat with Abby, Rocky walked into the Melchester Rovers dressing room. She was met with a roar.

"Can I play for you?" she asked.

Half the girls came over to Rocky, mobbing

her. The rest cheered and clapped. It was loud.

Loud, Rocky knew, because her old teammates wanted her new teammates from Mountain Heights to hear their victory.

Joining in, Rocky held up her Melchester Rovers top—a number 4 and her name ironed onto the back—and joined in the dance. Today—at least for this part of today—she was English. She was Melchester.

Melchester Rovers. The red and the yellow. The shirt and the colours she had been brought up on.

First with her dad being a massive fan, following them home and away, taking her and Roy to countless games. Posters up in her room. A pencil case at school. Everything had to be red and yellow.

Then her brother became a part of the Melchester Rovers men's team. Their captain, even, at the age of eighteen. It had been amazing for their family. Her brother had become the famous Roy of the Rovers.

And then Rocky—thanks to Ffion— becoming a player in the first Melchester

Rovers women's team while still a young teenager. A dream for her even greater than her brother being a player. Rocky would bleed red and yellow if they cut her open, she thought.

Then she felt slightly nauseous at the idea.

Perhaps just red.

Either way, wearing this shirt made Rocky feel good. Closer to home, her family, who she used to be. While, at the same time, being happy with who she was now. That was okay, wasn't it?

After the hullabaloo in the Melchester Rovers changing rooms, Rocky sat next to Ffion and they shared a smile.

"I have really, really missed playing alongside you," Ffion said. "Seeing you in those colours. I am so glad you're with us. It can't have been an easy choice."

"It wasn't," Rocky admitted, then leaned in. "Listen… can I ask you something?"

"Course."

Rocky was nervous about asking Ffion what she wanted to ask her. Ffion was a hero, a leader. It didn't feel right suggesting something that Ffion could do that wasn't Ffion's idea. But it had to be done, For Rocky. It was something she wanted to do, needed to do.

So, as the other players sorted their shinpads, tightened their boots and chatted excitedly about the game ahead, Rocky spoke softly to Ffion, then leaned back and watched her hero's face for a reaction.

Nine

THE GAME BEGAN as if the first minute was the last. Both teams going at it, end to end. None of that early play when teams sound each other out, probe for weaknesses, not taking any risks.

Mountain Heights deployed the long ball from the off, Kim with her back to goal, trapping the ball and trying to play in her wingers. Before the game was out of its first minute Ffion fouled Kim just outside the penalty area. The resulting free kick skimmed the top of the bar.

"Come on, USA!" someone in the crowd of student spectators shouted. Then more shouts. There were dozens of girls and boys watching, some with flags and banners bearing the Mountain Heights name.

"U-S-A! U-S-A!"

Rocky could see that her British teammates thought it was cheesy. And she understood how they felt. But she also kind of understood the American way, too.

After ten minutes, a foul the other way resulted in Ffion losing her boot. Naomi treading on the back of her heel. Ffion fell with the impact of the tackle and when she stood she was faced with Naomi holding her boot, a smirk on her face.

There was a definite edge to the game. Though—even though Rocky was the centre of this edge—no one had touched her yet.

"Can I have my boot back, please?" Ffion said in an angry voice, making sure Abby, as referee, heard her clearly.

"It's called a cleat," Naomi said, throwing the shoe to her. This drew laughs from her teammates.

"Boot."

"Cleat."

"Boot."

Abby stepped in. "Naomi, if it's on *your* foot, it's a cleat. If it's on *her* foot, it's a boot. Got it?"

Naomi looked a little surprised, but then nodded and jogged to her position.

Now Rocky stepped up to take the free kick that Ffion had won. She could tell there was more of an edge to the Mountain Heights team than her former teammates from Melchester. It didn't help that the Mountain Heights fans watching were chanting "U-S-A! U-S-A!" louder and louder.

She wanted more from Melchester Rovers. A competitive edge that was so far lacking. No one was putting fire in the bellies of the team.

She pointed at her badge and faced the English girls.

"Remember the badge?" she said, kissing it. "This badge. The history?"

"Proper history," Ffion shouted. "Hundreds of years of history!"

Now the Melchester players looked more focused. The vibe was changing.

The game went on, peppered with clashes and arguments about words.

Cleats, fields, soccer, scrimmage.

Boots, pitches, football, friendly.

It was tight. It was tense. There was no flow to the game. It was crying out for a goal. And that goal came from Kim.

Frustrated with how fragmentary play had become, she had begun to make fast short runs at the Melchester defence and now picked up a loose ball and just ran at it. Dodging two tackles she found space, drew the keeper and played the ball under her despairing dive. A classic solo goal. From nothing.

A huge cheer from the crowd.

"U-S-A! U-S-A!" again.

It was annoying. Rocky could see it on the faces of her Melchester teammates. Even she felt angry at all that USA stuff. It felt... not quite sporting, not fair. It almost made her want to stay on the pitch and fight for her old team.

But Abby had agreed to let her carry out her plan and Kim was involved now. Ffion, too. There was no going back. For now there were fifteen minutes left in the first half. Fifteen minutes Rocky wanted to give her all to.

Late in the half, with Abby already checking her watch, Rocky gathered an up-field throw in from Ffion, who had run the width of the pitch to take it, clearly frustrated by how the game was going, too.

Rocky saw Ffion run directly into the penalty area as soon as the throw was taken, shouldering between Naomi and Mahsa, even though she didn't need to. It was a statement of intent. A display of her passion. Ffion trying to wind up the opposition.

And Rocky remembered how she loved this about Ffion. How she had learned from her. This sort of thing. Combative play. Wind-up football. She was desperate for Ffion to have her moment. So Rocky turned, took two touches, drew Mahsa on the edge of the area, and slid a perfect pass between her two Mountain Heights teammate central defenders, Naomi and Mahsa. The pass had pace. The pass had accuracy. It arrived a metre ahead of Ffion, who, feinting to the right, slotted the ball to the left.

Goal.

1–1.

Rocky couldn't resist running to celebrate with Ffion, straight through the gap she and Ffion had exploited. She noted the look of rage on Naomi's face.

Hugging Ffion, Rocky wondered how the players on both teams were going to react to her plan. To what was going to happen next.

Ten

AFTER THE HALF-TIME drinks and coaching in huddles at either side of the pitch, Rocky caught Kim's eye. They both stood up at the same time and met in the centre circle.

"So, we're doing this?" Kim grinned.

"We are," Rocky confirmed.

"How do you think they'll react?" Kim asked, glancing at the Melchester players.

Rocky shrugged.

It felt strange as Rocky took off her Melchester Rovers top and handed it to Kim. Was it the last time she was going to wear it? On a football pitch? Even on a soccer field?

She took the Mountain Heights top from Kim and put it on. As her head emerged from the top of her shirt, she saw Kim doing the same. And was faced with her best friend wearing the shirt that meant so much to her.

Here was Kim in the red and yellow of Melchester Rovers.

"You look good in that," Rocky said.

"Well," Kim looked over her shoulder, "it's got my best friend's name and number on it."

The two friends smiled at each other.

"I know I am not supposed to say this because I am English and we don't gush... but I love you, Kim."

For a second Kim's face beamed, radiated happiness.

Then they heard Naomi shouting. "No. No. No... what are you doing?"

In the few moments Rocky and Kim had been smiling at each other, the players of both teams had moved in on them. They were surrounded.

"Swap back," Naomi demanded. "Kim's ours."

"And I'm not?" Rocky objected, noticing that Ffion was watching and smiling, keeping out of it.

"Well..." Naomi looked momentarily confused. "You're theirs, too. Sort of. I mean... we'll have you back. But Kim is ours. Why is she switching?"

Kim shook her head. "It's just for a half. And maybe it could be fun."

"What's fun about playing for the opposition?" Naomi said, exasperated. With more force. Angry again. "I don't get it. I don't... Abby? I mean... referee? They can't do this."

Voices from both teams protested. The crowd was booing. And Rocky smiled. She loved how wound up Naomi was being, how she and her Ghanaian friend had that in common.

"It's all agreed," Abby said, putting her lips to her referee's whistle. "It's a new training idea. Swapping players to challenge us. And, hey, what could be more challenging than that, Naomi?"

Rocky observed that Abby was laughing now. But she also saw that some of the other players were not...

Rocky did her best to be immediately

effective in the Mountain Heights team now she had switched over and the second half began. Back with her new teammates. It needed to be seamless.

But she could feel the confusion and—in some cases—anger at what she and Kim had done. Swapping shirts like that. Swapping loyalties?

Was it a good idea? she wondered. Would it backfire?

Then Rocky reminded herself of who she was. Remembered Jesse. What had he said to her last night when they'd had their conversation? *Just be yourself*, he had said. *You're a good footballer. You can slot into any team and improve it.*

Jesse was right. Rocky could do that.

So she took control. She protected her defenders, Mahsa and Naomi, turning to grin at them so they knew she was on their side now. Next, she played the ball up field to her forwards. This was who she was. This was what she did. This was what she was good at.

On the other team, Kim was playing as libero. A free-moving player, a forward with no fixed role. Ffion had not had time to decide or discuss what she should do. In doing so, she had dropped deeper.

And that meant it was Ffion versus Rocky in the centre of the pitch.

Rocky grinned.

Her aim now? To stifle Ffion. For forty-five minutes, to make the game so hard for Ffion that she got cross. If you stopped Ffion, you stopped Melchester Rovers. Nothing personal. It was football.

And for fifteen to twenty minutes Rocky achieved that. Tight and tough on Ffion. Suffocating her creativity. But then—in one moment Rocky knew she was capable of— Ffion took a ball, turned, shouldered past Rocky and, while falling, played a short ball up to Kim.

Knowing it was her fault Kim was away, Rocky went after her best friend.

Kim took two, then three touches and Rocky slid in to tackle. But it was too late. Kim had unleashed a fierce shot that smacked the underside of the bar and ricocheted into the net.

Kim jumped up and punched the air.

It was the best of goals.

But, since no one in the Melchester Rovers tops really knew Kim that well, the English girls didn't know quite how to congratulate her. But Rocky saw their mouths gaping open in awe at Kim's skill.

Rocky smiled. Maybe the English were a bit reserved. But it wasn't that they were stuck up. It was more respect, being unsure what the best way to behave was. Make sure they weren't offending Kim. Maybe? Who knew?

Seizing the moment, Rocky ran up to Kim and grabbed her, swung her round in celebration.

It was—for a second—a surreal scene. A player from one team congratulating a player from the other team for scoring, celebrating with her. But, after a pause of confusion, suddenly everyone was laughing. All over the pitch players hugging, high fiving.

Abby blew her whistle. "Back to the game," she said.

The players took up their positions, still

laughing. And the game went on, end to end.

Good humoured, but tough.

Mountain Heights needed a goal. Rocky knew that. This game had to end as a draw. Then the mood would stay good and she would feel okay if it ended in a draw… or a tie.

As the minutes ticked away—and even though players on both sides were still laughing—US players insisting on calling the field the pitch now and UK players shouting words like cleat and tie and scrimmage at every opportunity—Rocky was going into tackles with Ffion harder and harder.

"Still got it, then," Ffion laughed after she'd pulled Rocky down following a hard shoulder barge.

"Always," Rocky said.

The whistle blew. Free kick to Mountain Heights. Twenty yards out.

"Will you take it?" Rocky said, offering her shirt to Ffion. "Last kick leveller?"

A smile broke out on Ffion's face as she took off her Melchester top and slipped on the white.

"My pleasure."

There were cheers from the bleachers.

As Ffion lined up the free kick, Rocky noticed a Mountain Heights player going up to a Melchester player, grinning and offering to swap shirts. Then another. And another. There was laughter as all the players seemed to be changing sides.

This was good, Rocky thought. Now she understood the cheers.

Kim was standing next to Rocky now, arm round her shoulders.

Ffion took three steps back, stared at the ball, stared at the goal and the wall of players between them. Then she hit it. Hard. The keeper didn't even move.

Goal. 2–2.

Then Abby blew the final whistle.

"A tie," Rocky said.

"No," Kim said. "A draw."

And so to penalties.

Eleven

ROCKY LIKED PENALTY shoot-outs. She enjoyed the theatre of it. But also the way you had to just stand there and watch other people taking shots and there was nothing you could do, other than be positive for your teammates. Or try to get into the heads of the opposition.

It was a weird time where you had the opportunity to think. Just you and your thoughts. Nothing to do. No one really wanted to talk. You were just there with your thoughts. Between kicks.

Rocky smiled. *This* was the most bizarre shoot-out she'd been part of or even seen. All the players were wearing the shirts of the team they didn't play for.

But if they were wearing the shirts now, weren't they playing for them now? Who were they playing for? Who won if they scored and the players wearing the other shirts missed?

It was so confusing! Especially as everyone seemed to think it was hilarious.

And to make it more bizarre she could hear Naomi and Charlotte having an intense discussion—a friendly one—about whether it was fair or not to stare out the keeper, even say something to wind them up, before you took your kick. Then the two of them laughing.

This was a result! If Naomi and Charlotte were being light-hearted, there was hope for the universe.

Meanwhile the first two penalties went in.

So, the score was Mountain Heights 1, Melchester Rovers 1.

Rocky looked around the pitch, at the two lines of players getting ready for their shot. She noticed laughter and chat going on between both sides, saw players complimenting each other on their skills, saw Ffion and Kim gazing over at her and both smiling.

Even with the shoot-out score so tight, the vibe was great. That was the moment Rocky realised—to her shock—that her anxiety had gone. She stood with Kim on her left and Ffion on her right and she felt only good.

No tension.

It was nice. Sometimes it seemed to Rocky that feeling tense was just as much a part of her as feeling her breaths go in and out or her heart beating. But not now, not today.

The next two penalties were missed. The score remained Mountain Heights 1, Melchester Rovers 1.

Who am I? Rocky asked herself as she watched on. *What team do I belong to? And those worries I have? Do they matter?* She was here. That was all. And she was down to her undervest, having felt so hot she decided not to wear either team's top for now. So, she really was neither one nor the other.

Two more penalties went in. One for each

side. It was Mountain Heights 2, Melchester Rovers 2 now. After three shots each.

Next, two penalties were missed.

Then two scored.

3–3.

It went on like that. If a player in a Mountain Heights top scored, a player in a Melchester top scored, too. If they missed, the other side missed.

4–4.

5–5.

And then somehow—at 6–6—there was one player left who had yet to take a penalty.

Rocky.

Someone tossed the ball in her direction. She caught it with both hands, then walked towards the penalty spot, still in her undervest, giving off a Chloe Kelly vibe.

Two shirts were thrust at her.

"Wear this."

"No, this."

Then there was laughter, girls in white tops and red shorts with their arms round others in red tops and white shorts. And then noise. All twenty-plus players cheering her on.

Rocky shook her head, placed the ball on the penalty spot and changed her mind. It did matter.

Rocky stepped back. Two deep breaths. A third. Then a run up to the ball and she hit it.

Hard. Hard right. To the keeper's left.

And in.

Rocky found herself mobbed by both sets of players. She'd scored a winner. For all of them.

And those questions. The ones she'd been wrangling over for days. Was she Mountain Heights? Was she still Melchester? Whether she would be wearing red and yellow, or white with blue and yellow trim in three years? Or even playing in a Lioness shirt? What about that?

To be a Lioness?

That was her ultimate dream.

About the Author

Tom Palmer is a best-selling children's author from Leeds, England. He has written dozens of books for children, including the *Football Academy* series, and continues to inspire young readers up and down the UK. He supports Leeds United.

KICK OFF

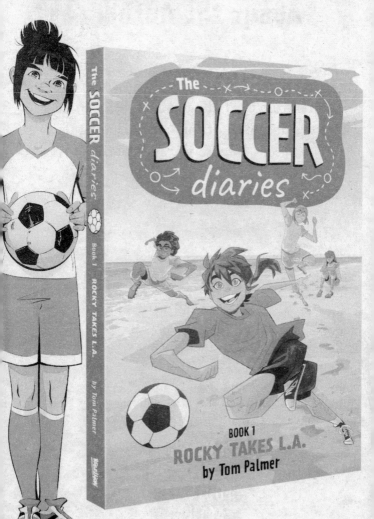

The SOCCER diaries

Book 1 — ROCKY TAKES L.A. — by Tom Palmer

The SOCCER diaries

BOOK 1
ROCKY TAKES L.A.
by Tom Palmer

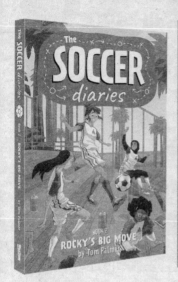

HAPPY WORLD BOOK DAY

Choosing to read in your free time can help make you:

Feel happier

Better at reading

More successful

Whether it's **comics**, **audiobooks**, **recipe books** or **non-fiction** you can visit your school, local library or nearest bookshop for your next read.

Keep the reading fun going by **swapping** this book, **talking** about it, or **reading it again!**

Discover more at worldbookday.com

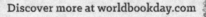

READ YOUR WAY

Celebrate World Book Day by reading
what YOU want in YOUR free time.

Have FUN
reading!

Take
books home
to read

Choose the
books you
want to read

Ask for ideas
on what to
read next

Make time
to read

Listen to
books being
read aloud

World Book Day® is a charity
sponsored by National Book Tokens.